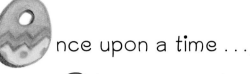nce upon a time . . .
there were **3** bears named "Brown"
who lived in the town of

LEO was the papa, **IRMA** was the mama, and **PATRICK** was the little boy.

For Maureen Sullivan

Printed in Singapore

First Edition

1 3 5 7 9 10 8 6 4 2

This book was set in Tweed Medium 19.

Library of Congress Cataloging-in-Publication Data
Hayes, Geoffrey.
Patrick at the circus / story and pictures by Geoffrey Hayes.—1st ed.
p.   cm.
Summary: Patrick the bear watches his father's clown performance at the circus.
ISBN 0-7868-0716-4 (hc)
[1. Circus—Fiction. 2. Clowns—Fiction. 3. Bears—Fiction.]
PZ7.H31455 Parv 2002
[E]—dc21
2001039078

Visit www.hyperionchildrensbooks.com

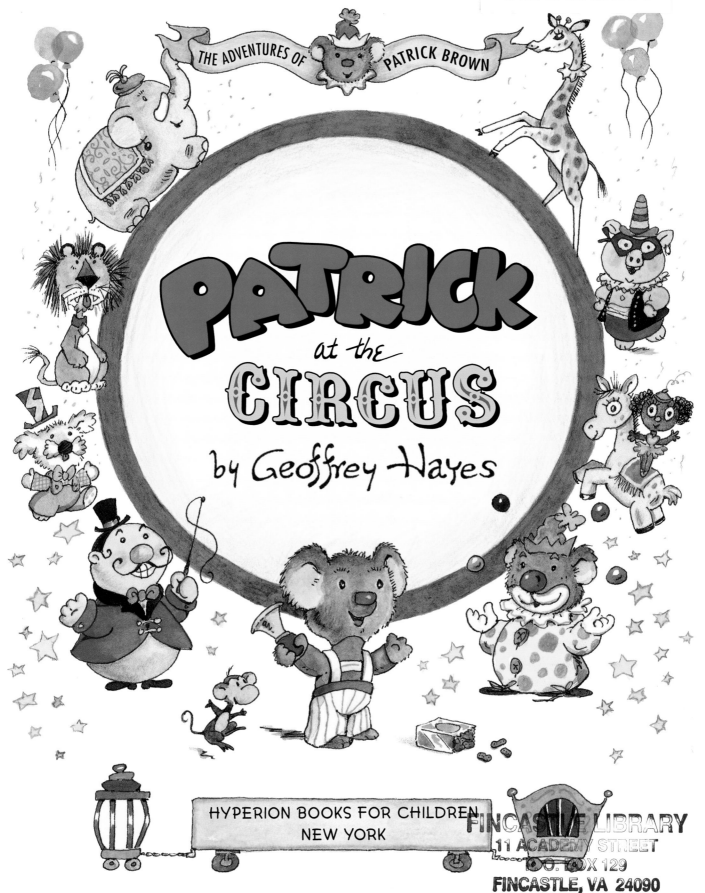

THE ADVENTURES OF PATRICK BROWN

PATRICK
at the
CIRCUS

by Geoffrey Hayes

HYPERION BOOKS FOR CHILDREN
NEW YORK

The circus was coming to town!
"I've never been to the circus before,"
said Patrick. "Not in my WHOLE life!
Can we go, Mama . . . please?"
"Of course we can," said Mama Bear.

Mrs. Brown, I have a book about the circus.

"The circus is where I first met your father."

"Was he a LION TAMER?"
asked Patrick.

"No," said Mama,
"a **CLOWN**...
I always knew I was going
to marry either a clown
or a fireman.

"I figured I'd get
plenty of laughs with
a clown ... and I have."

"Papa, were you
really a clown?"

"Was I ever!"
said Papa.

In the attic, Papa scuffled about until he found an old poster with his picture on it. "That's me," he said. "ALWAYS LEAVE 'EM LAUGHING BROWN." He found his clown costume . . . GOOD AS NEW!

They tiptoed down to the kitchen.

HONK!

"Once a clown, always a clown!" said Papa.

Oh, you!

"Let's join the circus," cried Patrick.
"Then I can be a clown, too!"

"You're some clown already!" answered Mama. "Besides, you have to go to SCHOOL first."

"I do not!"

Papa said, "Patrick, being a circus performer takes lots of practice and hard work. Tomorrow, when we go to the circus, you will see for yourself."

The next morning, Patrick and Papa woke up early so they could go over to **NOBODY'S FIELD** and watch the circus tent go up.

The RINKO SISTERS wanted to come along.

So did WEAVER BEAR . . .

and TED.

Soon, the tent rose above the field, bright and big and beautiful!

Patrick and Papa
didn't see the little
monkey sneaking
up behind them
until it was . . .

That naughty monkey
stole Papa's wallet!

Patrick and Papa chased
the monkey all over
the circus grounds.

MISS JEWEL

Just when they had him cornered up the giraffe, the Ringmaster ran over, calling:

Come down from there, you little imp!

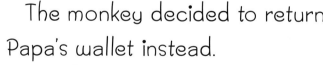

The monkey decided to return Papa's wallet instead.

CONK!

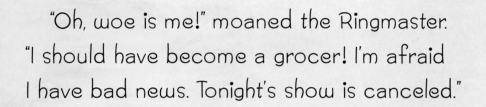

"Oh, woe is me!" moaned the Ringmaster. "I should have become a grocer! I'm afraid I have bad news. Tonight's show is canceled."

"But it **can't** be!" cried Patrick. "Sorry," said the Ringmaster. "You see, the clown just quit. And a circus simply isn't a circus without a clown."

I'm tired of being laughed at!

"Wait a minute!" cried Papa Bear.
"I'M a clown! Why not let me do it?"

"He's ALWAYS LEAVE
'EM LAUGHING BROWN!"
said Patrick.

The Ringmaster jumped for joy.
"What a splendid idea, Mr. Brown! Thank you.
A good clown is hard to find these days."
He pulled a bunch of tickets from his pocket and gave
them to Papa. "Here, invite all your friends. Tonight's on me!"

Papa and Patrick hurried home to tell Mama the good news.
Papa was so excited he juggled a few household items—
just for fun—and he didn't drop a single one!

"Mama, watch MY circus act,"
said Patrick.

"Later, love," Mama replied. "I have
to help Papa get ready for tonight."

"Just watch this ONE part."

"Patrick, why don't you practice in the yard for a while?" said Papa.

"NO," cried Patrick. "I can DO it!"

He kicked over a chair . . .

and was told
to go outside—
PRONTO!

"Dumb Papa!" said Patrick.
"I can be funny, too!"

Patrick stayed outside all afternoon.
When Papa Bear left for the circus,
Mama said, "Patrick, you've been waiting
to see the circus your whole life. You'll
spoil things if you're grumpy."

"I DON'T CARE," said Patrick.

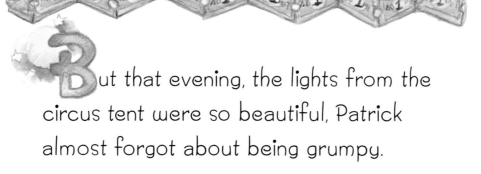

But that evening, the lights from the
circus tent were so beautiful, Patrick
almost forgot about being grumpy.

Patrick and Mama got seats in the very first row.
The organ-grinder pig played a happy melody.
YIPPY, the little dog, sold peanuts.

When all the seats were full, the lights dimmed, the drums rolled, and the Ringmaster appeared in the spotlight.

First up was MISS JEWEL, who drank a glass of water while hanging upside down. Below . . .

ELLY ELEPHANT performed feats of strength.

HE'S ELEPHAN-TASTIC!

"Do you think Papa is coming out next?" asked Mama.

"I DON'T CARE," said Patrick.

The Ringmaster called:

"Ladies and gentlemen and little kids, presenting the **M**ean and **H**orrible, **T**errible, **F**erocious LION!"

A cage was wheeled out and the lion was released.

The Ringmaster changed into his lion-tamer's hat, cracked his whip, and made the lion perform tricks.

The lion pretended to be angry. He caught the Ringmaster's whip between his teeth and ran in circles around the ring.

"I'm scared, Mama," said Patrick.
"Don't worry," Mama replied.
"The lion is nothing but a big kitty."

Suddenly, a little clown with a firehose raced out from the sidelines. It was ALWAYS LEAVE 'EM LAUGHING BROWN!

POOM!

He was so busy waving to everybody, he tripped over his big shoes and fell smack on his nose.

WAS HE HURT?

NO! It was just part of the act.

GROWL!

Now the lion chased
PAPA around the ring.

Papa leaped through a hoop of fire.

Well, what do you know?
It was only FAKE fire!

"Isn't he wonderful!" cried Patrick.

Just then, Papa dropped his clown hat and the naughty monkey made off with it.

Before Mama could stop him, Patrick ran into the ring, calling:

Let go of my papa's hat, you little imp!

Patrick chased the monkey around poles and over drums as the crowd roared with laughter.

Finally, Elly Elephant managed to get Papa's hat away from the monkey. He tossed it to Miss Jewel,

who tossed it to Patrick . . .

. . . and Patrick caught it!

"Here, Papa," he said. "You dropped your hat."
Papa placed the hat on PATRICK'S head.
More drums rolled.

And Patrick got to ride high on Papa's shoulders in the **GRAND FINALE** — just like a circus star!

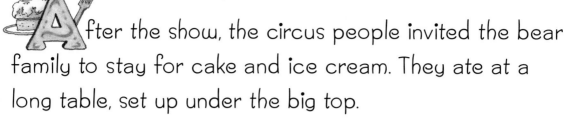

After the show, the circus people invited the bear family to stay for cake and ice cream. They ate at a long table, set up under the big top.

"A toast!" called the Ringmaster. "To ALWAYS LEAVE 'EM LAUGHING BROWN and his partner, LITTLE LEAVE 'EM LAUGHING BROWN!"

Later, Mama, Papa, and Patrick strolled home in the moonlight.

"I like circus people," said Papa.

"I do, too," said Mama.

"Once a clown, always a clown,"
said Patrick.

"Oh, you," said Mama. Then she
gave BOTH her clowns a great big hug.

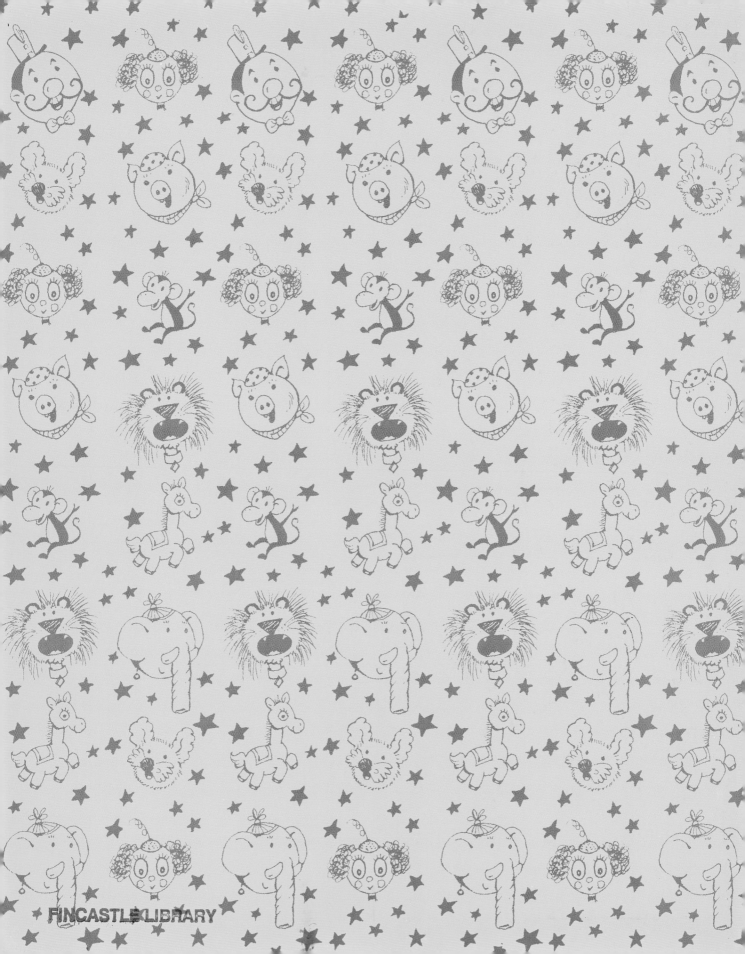